THE MONSTER BIRTHDAY PARTY

BY CAROLYN DINAN

KU-243-452

Hamish Hamilton · London

UNIVERSITY OF CENTRAL ENGLAND INFORMATION SERVICES

UNIVERSITY OF
CENTRAL ENGLAND

Book no. 0806 5012

Subject no.   JJ Din

INFORMATI   RVICES

It was the night before Tom's birthday.

He woke up in the dark and found a mysterious box beside his bed. The label said:

DO NOT OPEN BEFORE
YOUR BIRTHDAY

"It is my birthday," said Tom. "Well, nearly."

"A monster!" Tom shouted, opening the box.

"If you don't mind," said the monster, "my name is Steg. I'm inviting you to my birthday party."

"Great!" said Tom. "How do we get there?"

"Easy," said Steg. "Just get in the box."

So Tom put on his green monster slippers and jumped in.

The box was much bigger than Tom thought. He couldn't feel the sides. It was a long time before his feet touched the ground.

"Steg," he said, "I can't see a thing in here!"

"It's getting lighter now," said Steg. "Look."

Tom saw a huge green shape towering over him.

"Steg!" gasped Tom. "You've grown."
"Have I?" asked Steg. "I'm usually this sort of size. Maybe you've shrunk. There's something funny about that box."

"Where is the box?" Tom said. "Where are we?"

"We're in my kitchen," said Steg proudly. "Come and meet my family. Ma will think you're lovely!"

Tom soon made friends with Meg and little Tig.

But Ma didn't think Tom was lovely at all.

"Oh dear," said Steg. "I forgot she's scared of little wiggly things."

"Never mind," said Meg. "Come and see our room."
After that they crept into Ma's room.

"I'll just show Tom Ma's jewels," said Steg.
They ran into the bathroom. Steg forgot all about
Ma's ring on his paw. Down the plug-hole it went!

"I'll go down the pipe for it," said Tom bravely.

So Meg unscrewed the cover on the plug-hole.

Steg tied thread around Tom's waist and gently lowered him.

"Don't worry. I'll find it for you," said Tom.

And he did. They put the ring safely back in its box, just as the doorbell rang.

The guests had arrived! Steg ripped open his presents all at once. Tom kept very still so no one would notice him. And no one did till Ma rushed in.

She whisked Tom off the table and held him up.
"Quiet, please, little monsters. Hide your eyes.
We're playing 'Hunt the Caveman'. Whoever
finds him first is the winner."

Steg was not a good hunter.

"He'll never find me," muttered Tom. "But someone else will, any minute. Help!"

Suddenly, a stripey monster pounced on Tom.

"Steg!" yelled Tom. "Over here!"

"I'm coming," shouted Steg. "Out of my way, everyone." And he snatched Tom out of the stripey monster's paw.

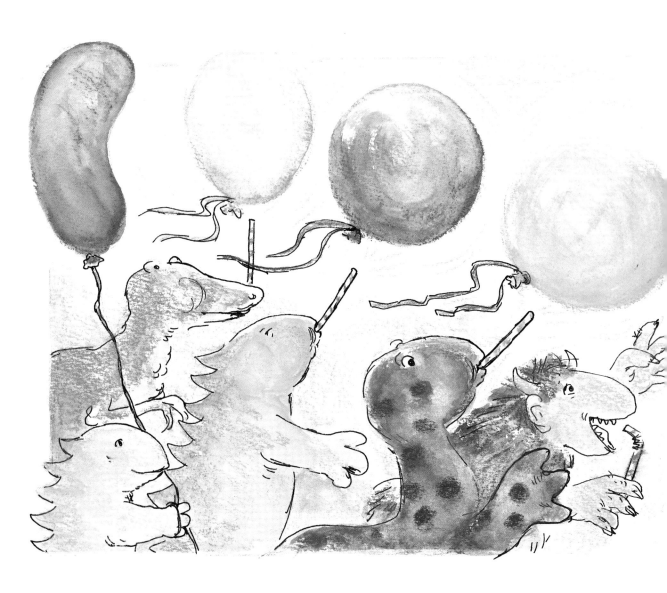

"Right, Tom. Now for some fun," said Steg.

All the monsters loved the Balloon Race. Tom swung from Steg's balloon in his monster slippers with the sharp black claws.

No one saw, but one by one all the balloons burst.

BANG! BANG! BANG!

All except Steg's!

Meg was cross. "It's rude to win all the games at
your own party, Steg," she said.

"Sorry," said Steg. "Let's play 'Hide and Seek'.
I'll be the finder so it's quite safe, Tom."

"I'd better go home after that. It must be my
own birthday by now," said Tom.

Steg closed his eyes and counted to a hundred.

"Put me on the table, Meg," said Tom. "I know a good place to hide."

He propped a drinking straw against Steg's birthday cake and shinned up it on to the top.

In the middle of the cake stood a velvety-green toy monster. Somehow he seemed familiar.

"You're just the right size to hide behind," said Tom.

Tom waited and waited. Suddenly there was a blaze of light. Ma was lighting the candles!

"Happy Birthday, Steg," she beamed. "Make a wish, and…oh no! What's that on your cake?"

Meg turned out the lights. "Quick," she whispered. "Blow out the candles, Steg, and wish Tom safely home."

Steg took a deep breath and blew out all the candles. Tom sailed off the cake, out into the dark. Far away he could hear the monsters singing:

"Happy Birthday dear To-om,
Happy Birthday to you."
"But it's Steg's party," said Tom. And then he landed with a thump.

"Happy Birthday to you," sang Tom's mum. "You've already opened your present!"

Tom looked at the toy monster tucked up in his bed. I suppose I just dreamed it all, he thought sadly.

Tom's mum stared at him. "Why are you wearing your slippers in bed? And what have you got on them? It looks like icing! What have you been up to, Tom?"

"Lots!" he said, patting the green monster. "I'm naming him 'Steg'. And Mum! Don't throw the box away!"

"We'll keep it safe," Mum promised. "It might come in useful one day."

"It will," said Tom, and he winked at Steg. And, just for a moment, he thought Steg winked back.